WITCH WAY TO JINGLE

MAGICAL MOJO BOOK 2

DAWN SULLIVAN

All rights reserved. No part of this publication may be reproduced, stored in a retrieval system, or transmitted in any form or by means mechanical, electronic, photocopying, recording, or otherwise without prior permission from the author. This is a work of fiction. Names, characters, places, and events are fictitious in every regard. Any similarities to actual events or persons, living or dead, are purely coincidental. Any trademarks, service marks, product names, or featured names are assumed to be the property of their respective owners and are used only for reference. There is no implied endorsement of any of these terms used. Except for review purposes, the reproduction of this book in whole or in part, mechanically or electronically, constitutes a copyright violation. Published in the United States of America in January 2021; Copyright 2021 by Dawn Sullivan. The right of the Author's Name to be identified as the Author of the Work has been asserted by them in accordance with The Copyright, Designs, and Patent Act of 1988.

Published by Dawn Sullivan

Cover Design: T. E. Black Designs

Editors: Ryder Editing and Formatting

Copyright 2021 © Author Dawn Sullivan

Language: English

WITCH WAY TO JINGLE

Willow Ryder is a strong, self-confident witch who is content to live her life just the way it is. Safe. She has her job as a prominent attorney with a well-known law firm and her coven. She doesn't need anything else. Well, except maybe to have a little fun at her neighbor's expense, the cheating bastard.

Dominic Hamilton has known since he was a teenager that he was meant to live life alone. While it might be a lonely existence, he doesn't believe he deserves love and happiness after what happened years ago. As long as his family is happy, that's all he needs to make it through.

When Dom and Willow's paths cross one night, they both try to avoid a destiny that's been decided for them. Fate may have chosen them to be together, but there is no way that is ever going to happen. The Goddess above has no idea what she is doing… or does she?

When danger threatens the life Willow has made for herself and all the things that hold her heart, she comes to realize that it is time she must decide witch way to jingle.

CHAPTER ONE

Willow concentrated on the tree branches directly above the bright red wannabe sports car. A slow smile appeared when they began to shake and groan, before dumping what had to be a foot of snow on top of the vehicle. After a quick glance around, she began to mutter a low chant, watching in satisfaction as the snow started to melt over the car, and then freeze when she altered the words in the spell.

Soon, the small car looked like it was encased in a huge ice cube, and Willow couldn't stop the laughter that escaped as she grabbed the newspaper off her front steps and turned and went back into her house. Served the bastard right for cheating on his wife. There was no way they would be able to get the Mazda unthawed and out of there before the Mrs. came home from her night shift at the hospital in a couple of hours. She wished she could see the look on her husband's face when he was caught with his pants down… in a manner of speaking.

Willow paused in the entryway, cocking her head to the

side, another burst of laughter hitting her. Maybe she *could* watch it all unfold. She was sure she could conjure a spell for that, and it just might be worth the time it would take to figure it out. Maybe she should call over a few of her coven sisters for some popcorn and to watch the show.

Chuckling to herself, she made her way into the kitchen. Tossing the paper on the island, she wandered over to make some coffee, while she contemplated the wording she would need to use to pull up the scene that would soon be unravelling next door, and slap it on her big screen TV in the basement.

Her Keurig was humming, the smell of French Vanilla filling the air, and Willow had just reached for her phone to call her best friend Desi, when it began to ring. Sighing, she glanced at the caller ID, expecting it to be the office, even though they'd promised her the next three weeks off. She'd been working like a damn dog the entire year, and just needed some time to unwind, but the partners she worked for at Johnson and Johnson Law Firm didn't see it that way. They expected her to be at their beck and call, and she had been ever since she started there after passing the bar exam eight years ago. But if she didn't get some time away from the place she was beginning to think of as 'Hell' soon, she was going to blow a gasket.

Willow gritted her teeth together tightly when she was proven right, and one of the partner's numbers flashed across the phone. Not just any partner, but the one who had been trying to get her into his bed for the past six months. She had managed to avoid his advances so far, but he was getting more and more persistent, and it was really starting to piss her off.

She contemplated ignoring the call, but knew she

couldn't. She was on track to making partner in the company, hopefully within the next year. If she wanted that to happen, she needed to be available to them twenty-four seven, even on her days off. All three weeks of it.

Cursing under her breath, she answered, "Willow Ryder."

There was a slight pause, and then Derek Johnson's voice came over the line. "Sorry to interrupt your vacation, Willow."

Bullshit. The slimy bastard didn't care at all what he was interrupting. As grandson to the owner of the law firm, he thought he was entitled to everyone's time, no matter who it was.

"Willow?"

"I'm here." That was all she gave him. She had no desire to speak with him, now or ever, but she would out of respect for his grandfather… and because she really wanted to make partner in the company.

"Look, I was hoping you could come in and help out on a case of mine. I need to go out of town for a week or two."

What he really meant was that he was going on his yearly skiing trip in Colorado with his frat buddies from college. The same one he went on yearly since he graduated. She had to listen to the stories of his escapades every January when he returned—a man who was now in his forties, preying on women way younger than he was.

"Find someone else."

"Ah, Willow, come on. There isn't anyone as good as you, and this case is going to be difficult."

A part of her was intrigued at the word *difficult*, but not enough to take the bait. Not this time.

"I'm sure Brandon or Christopher can handle it."

"They aren't you," Derek said, in a wheedling tone that grated on her nerves. "And they have their own cases going right now."

"Not my problem," Willow snapped before she could control herself, and instantly regretted letting her anger take over. Inhaling deeply, she calmed herself before saying, "Look, Derek, I was promised a full three weeks off with no phone calls and no cases. I intend to take those three weeks. If you need to call to get my opinion on something, or you have a question relating to one of *my* cases, I would be happy to help. Otherwise, I would appreciate being able to take the time I was given without interruption."

There was silence, and then... "You could always come with me."

"What?" Go with him and his loser college buddies? Was he crazy?

"Come on, Willow," Derek said smoothly, and she could picture that slimy smile of his crossing his face. "Come with me. We'll do some skiing during the day, have candlelight dinners at night, and talk about our future."

Willow's eyebrows arched so high at the last sentence; she was surprised they were still on her forehead. "Tell me, Derek, just what future might that be?"

"One that includes the two of us spending the rest of our lives together."

Willow's hand tightened on the phone, her mouth opening in shock. Was he seriously hinting at what she thought he was? No way in hell was she spending her life with a player like Derek Johnson. That man would never settle down. She would end up like the sad story that was taking place across the street. Not going to happen. She didn't need a man, especially not one like him.

A pair of striking blue eyes flashed through her mind, along with a strong curve of a jaw and a dimple that appeared when a sexy, wicked grin crossed his face. Dominic Hamilton, the one person who the Goddess had supposedly chosen for her—if she was to believe the stories Desi had told her about how she and Drake had been drawn to each other. Dominic was the man Willow had been avoiding as much as possible since the night they'd met.

Willow firmly shut the door on those thoughts, bringing her attention back to the man who was currently spewing what he thought was convincing words in her ear. Running a hand through her thick hair, she interrupted him. "Derek, I don't know what you think is going on between us but let me reiterate what I have already told you several times. I am not now, nor will I ever be, interested in anything more from you than a working relationship. I do not fraternize with anyone outside of the workplace, no matter who it is. I keep my work life separate from my private life. So, that being said, thank you for the invitation, but I am going to politely decline. Now, I'm going back to my vacation. Have a nice day."

Ignoring his sputtering, she hung up the phone, praying she hadn't ruined any chances of further advancement in the company. Unfortunately, it had come to a point where she might have to choose her sanity over her job. She honestly didn't know if she could handle another case right now, no matter what it was. The eighty hours a week she'd been working since the beginning of the year was taking a toll on her, and her stress level was through the roof. She was on edge constantly, losing control of the rage that had been building inside her for months now, and doing stupid things like popping the neighbor's tires on his car the other day before he could leave for work, and encasing his tramp's car in ice that morning. Although she amused herself by doing those things, it was also spurred by her anger.

No sooner had the thought crossed Willow's mind, than she saw his wife's SUV making its way down the street out of the edge of her kitchen window. She was home early!

Grabbing her coffee, she rushed through the kitchen to get a better view out of the huge picture window in her living room. Willow took her first sip of the lifesaving brew in her hands as she watched the scene begin to unfold outside. The wife didn't have to go in the house to find out what a cheating bastard her husband was. He was outside, dressed only in his bathrobe and a pair of snow boots with his tramp of a girlfriend, frantically trying to beat the ice off her little Miata. Ice that wasn't budging. It looked like she wasn't going to have to conjure a spell to watch it on her television after all. It was going to take place right outside in front of her house.

The wife pulled slowly into the driveway, opened the garage door, and drove in. Soon, she was stalking out toward them, halting a few feet away and crossing her arms over her chest as she glared at her husband. He stopped what he was doing to look over at her, guilt all over his face.

Holding out his arms in a placating manner, he started to plead his case. Willow took another sip of her coffee as she watched the woman arch an eyebrow while she listened. She couldn't hear what was being said, but that was almost better, because she could imagine her own commentary in her mind. Right now, she was thinking that the husband was begging for one more try. The side hoe had stopped banging on her car and was now staring at him, a mutinous look on her face. She was pissed off and looked like she was about to put her two cents' worth in.

The wife waited a moment, letting him say his piece, and then unfolded her arms, took a step forward, and kneed him in the junk. Willow choked on her coffee when the man fell to the ground in pain, moaning as he cupped his crotch in his hands. His wife showed no compassion, turning and leaving him and the other woman where they were as she went inside the house, slamming the door behind her.

Deciding she'd had enough fun for the day, Willow concentrated on the car and began to whisper softly. Soon, the ice was gone as if it had never been there. The girlfriend was yelling at the poor asshole who was now crying as he held his dick. But, as soon as she saw her car was miraculously free of ice, she shut up, her gaze going around the area nervously. Willow knew the moment when the woman saw her but couldn't find it in herself to care.

After one last look, Willow raised her hand and waved her fingers at the couple who were now both staring in open-mouthed shock at her, before turning and walking away from the window. They might think she had something to do with what had just happened, but they would never know for sure. She liked the thought of keeping them wondering. And maybe, just maybe, they were both a little terrified of her now. She shrugged. Oh well. If they were, they deserved it.

CHAPTER TWO

Two weeks. It had been two long weeks since he last saw her. Two weeks and five days, if you wanted to be exact. He was so damn tired. He couldn't sleep. Every time he tried to get some rest; her image filled his mind. Those beautiful, dark green eyes that flashed fire when she was irritated, which she almost always was around him. Her pert little nose, and those full, luscious lips that she loved to paint dark red. That long, bright blue hair that on anyone else, he would think looked ridiculous, but not on her. No, his Willow could pull off any color of hair.

Fuck, *his* Willow.

He didn't want a woman to claim as his own. Didn't deserve one. Not after what happened so long ago. Shame filled him, grief swamping him at the thought of everything he'd lost that night. Because of his own stupid actions. His two best friends, gone.

He just wanted to live his life in peace. Alone. But, for some reason, the Goddess had chosen him, thinking he was worthy of someone as strong and beautiful as Willow. She was wrong. He wasn't even close to her equal. She was so much better than he would ever be.

Dominic groaned, rubbing his hand over the place where his heart beat erratically in his chest. It physically hurt to be separated from his witch. It was an empty, aching feeling, as if he wasn't complete without Willow in his life.

Why the hell had the Goddess chosen them to be together?

"Dom?"

Dominic looked up to see his grandmother standing in front of him, his brow furrowing as he wondered how long she'd been there. Raking a hand through his hair, he looked around in confusion. He sat in one of the chairs in their large living room that his mother had clearly picked out by looks, and not how comfortable they were. The lights were off, and the heavy drapes were shut tightly, so he had no idea what time it was.

"It's only going to get worse."

Rubbing a hand over his face, he asked gruffly, "What do you mean, Grandma?"

"Until you wake up and accept your fate, things are only going to get worse."

Dominic met her gaze, shaking his head. As much as he wanted to, he couldn't do it.

Before he could reply, Victoria held up her hand. "Stop, right now, Dominic Roland Hamilton. Lie to yourself if you want to, but do not lie to me. Ever."

Dominic bowed his head in shame, his eyes closing in exhaustion. "Sorry, Grandma."

Victoria was quiet for a long time, before she asked softly, "Do you not want the woman the Goddess has chosen for you, Dom? Is that it?"

He didn't want to talk about this to anyone, not even his grandmother. It hurt too much. All of it.

"You know the Goddess doesn't make mistakes."

"She did this time," he muttered.

"Give it some time," Victoria suggested, placing a hand gently on his shoulder. "Get to know Willow. She may be headstrong and... feisty..."

Dominic snorted. His witch was definitely those things, and so much more. Then what his grandmother said sank in. His head snapped up, his eyes narrowing on her. "How did you know?"

"That Willow holds the other half of your heart?"

"No one holds my heart," he said gruffly, unable to stop the glare he sent her way.

"That her magic calls to yours?" his grandmother went on, ignoring his response. "That your souls call to one another?"

"My soul, heart, and magic belong to me alone."

Victoria's eyes widened, then darkened in anger. "You would deny her? Leave her alone for the rest of her life? For eternity?"

Dominic frowned, shaking his head. "It's not like she's in a hurry to claim me either, Grandma."

"Yeah, I wouldn't want to jump on the Dom train right now either, the way you've been acting," Desi said, as she strode into the room, giving Victoria a quick smile.

"Seriously?" Drake was right behind her, where he always was. The two were hardly ever apart anymore. "Did you seriously just say *the Dom train*?"

Desi shrugged, glancing back at him. "You can't argue with me. He's had several chances to talk to Willow but hasn't done more than say stupid shit to antagonize her since they met."

"Wait," Dominic said, holding up a hand as he tried to keep up with the conversation. His eyes were blurring, his head pounding, and he was finding it hard to pay attention. "You told me to stay away from her. You don't want me near her."

"I did," Desi agreed, sending his brother a glance that Dominic found hard to decipher. "But that was then, this is now."

"Why?" He couldn't get anymore than that one word out. His head felt so heavy, he could hardly keep it up to look at them.

"Because, Dom," Desi said, kneeling down beside his chair and meeting his gaze. "I care about you both, and I want to see you as happy as we are."

"That will never happen," he muttered, trying to pry open eyes that had somehow drifted shut.

"Why not?"

Dominic heard the confusion in his sister-in-law's voice, but couldn't say anything more than a muttered, "Don't deserve her."

"What's he talking about?" Desi demanded loudly.

"Let's get you to bed, Brother."

Dominic grunted when Drake hauled him up out of the chair and threw him over his shoulder like a sack of potatoes in one smooth motion, but was unable to say a word.

"Drake, what did he mean by that?"

"I'll explain later."

No! He didn't need others knowing about that night. It

was his personal demon. His cross to bear. His secret, dammit!

Dominic felt Drake drop him on his bed, and someone removed his shoes.

"Maybe the spell was too powerful?"

What? What spell?

"Naw, Dom's just really tired, sweetheart."

His fucking brother had used a spell on him? Inside, Dominic seethed with anger, but he was unable to speak or even move. There was going to be hell to pay when he could, though. He and Drake had made a pact a long time ago to never use their magic on each other, unless it was in dire circumstances.

"He's going to be angry when he wakes up." It was his grandmother's voice, and she sounded more matter-of-fact than worried.

"Well, we'll let him think I was the one who turned him into Sleeping Beauty, so he doesn't turn that anger on you, Grandma."

Wait, a minute. It was his *grandmother* who knocked his ass out?

"Let him know it was me," Victoria said. "Little shit deserves it after what he plans on putting that young woman through."

What?

Dominic fought to stay lucid. He needed to know what his grandmother meant. What was he planning on putting Willow through? The only thing he was going to do was stay away from her so that she had a chance at a better life than she would ever have with someone like him.

"Go home, Desi. I'll stay with my brother."

That was the last thing Dominic heard before he succumbed to the darkness that was calling to him.

CHAPTER THREE

"Oh, my Goddess!" Tilly gasped, tears streaming down her cheeks as she giggled uncontrollably. "I can't believe you turned the toy Miata into an ice freaking cube! That's golden!"

"What happened after you unthawed the car?" Arabella asked, her golden-brown eyes lit with laughter.

"I have no idea," Willow said with a shrug.

"None at all?" Desi asked, arching an eyebrow in disbelief.

Willow let a grin spread across her face, knowing her eyes were filled with mischief as she replied, "Well, I may have peeked out the window a little later and I might have seen the wife throwing some clothes out on the lawn."

"And?" Raelyn took a draw from her beer as she waited for Willow to continue.

Willow glanced around at the women—her coven and laughed. "Fine. The girlfriend…"

"Miss Trampy Tramp herself," Calla cut in, sticking her tongue out.

"The one and only," Willow agreed. "She'd already left, but the man was banging on the front door begging his wife to let him in, as she was throwing his clothes out of an upstairs window."

"And?" Leighton encouraged, shoving some popcorn into her mouth?

"Well, he finally gave up on trying to get inside, and went to get some clothes to put on." Willow looked over at the Christmas movie that was playing on her seventy-five-inch television, biting her bottom lip, before she said, "Let's just say, the poor man had a hard time capturing the clothing that was flying all over the yard."

"You didn't!" Brinley cried, her loud giggles ringing out in the room. "I would have paid to see that!"

"Poor man, my ass," Desi said, taking a sip of her white wine. "Stupid fool, if you ask me."

"I agree."

Willow swallowed hard, moving a hand up to lightly rub over the pain in her chest, right over her heart. It had started a couple of months ago, the night she met Dominic Hamilton. She knew what it was—what it meant. Desi had explained it to her. She also knew the only way it would go away was after they completed their bond, one designated by the Goddess herself. That didn't mean she had to follow through with it. Hell, the man was frustrating and didn't even hardly talk to her, much less act like he wanted to spend the rest of his life together, which was just fine with her. Even if it hurt, both physically and emotionally.

"You okay?" Desi asked softly, while the others continued to joke about what had taken place the day before. When Willow looked over at her, but didn't reply,

Desi lowered her eyes to where Willow was still rubbing at that ache over her heart.

Willow let her hand fall to her lap, looking back over at the TV. "Yes."

"Liar."

Willow shook her head, not wanting to discuss it in front of the others. They were all her sisters, but she wasn't ready to share this with them.

"This has gone on long enough, Willow. We're talking tonight."

Before Willow could say anything else, like tell her bestie to mind her own damn business, there was a loud knock on the door upstairs. She jumped up, grateful for the distraction, and set her bottle of beer on the coaster beside her half empty bucket of popcorn. "I'll be right back."

"You aren't getting out of this," Desi called out, her voice trailing behind Willow as she ran up the stairs.

She made it to the door in record time, opening it without bothering to check who was on the other side first, and froze. "What are you doing here?" Her question was abrupt and to the point, but seriously, couldn't she catch a break? All she'd asked for was a few weeks off. That was it. Obviously, it was too much.

Derek Johnson stood on her front porch steps, dressed to the nines in a black tuxedo and shoes that looked like they'd been spit shined. He gave her what she was sure he considered a bashful grin, but it just made her skin crawl. "Hey."

Crossing her arms over her chest, she raised her eyebrows and asked again, "What are you doing here, Derek?"

This was her home. Her happy fucking place. *Hers*. No

one came here unless she invited them, and he hadn't been invited.

"I just wanted to see you, Willow." Shoving his hands in his front pockets, he lifted his shoulders in a small shrug. "Is that so hard to believe?"

"Yes."

Willow was aware of Desi coming up behind her and watched Derek's reaction when his gaze left hers to go to her friend. His eyes widened, along with his grin. Cocking his head to the side, he said, "Well, hello there. I'm Attorney Derek Johnson. And you are?"

"Married to a billionaire," Desi said dryly, ignoring the hand Derek held out to her. "Willow, Drake just called. He and Dom are going out and would like us to meet up with them. You in?"

Willow stiffened at the mention of Dominic, her heart beginning to race. She hadn't seen the man who supposedly was meant for her in a long time. Not since the end of November. Did she want to see him? The answer was an easy one, even though she knew it shouldn't be.

"Yep."

"Where are you going?" Derek interrupted. "I'd love to come."

"Sorry, but it would be kind of strange to take you on a date with us," Desi said, giving him a tight smile as she grasped Willow's upper arm and tugged her back so she could shut the door.

"Wait! I came here to talk to Willow."

"Sorry, she's busy." No sooner did the words leave Desi's mouth, than she slammed the door in Derek's surprised face.

"Come on, Willow," Derek called out, as Desi turned

both the lock on the doorknob and the deadbolt. "Let's talk about this."

When Desi turned to look at her, as if asking silently if she really wanted to talk to the man, Willow shook her head and mouthed, "Let's go."

Nodding, Desi made her way down the hall toward the back door where their coven sisters now stood, putting on their coats.

"Who's riding with who?" Willow asked, grabbing her white parka and slipping her arms into the puffy sleeves. She slid her feet into dark brown boots that came up to just beneath her knees next and then grabbed the keys that hung next to the door.

"We're going to take my car," Desi said, shrugging into her own coat. "I parked on the street behind your house. Everyone else is going home, so they'll take their own vehicles."

"What? Wait, a minute. I assumed we were all going together."

Desi shook her head as she slid on a pair of gloves. "Nope, you're stuck with me. They all have better things to do."

"Like what?" Willow argued, glaring at the other women.

"Like sleep," Arabella said, giving Willow a quick hug. "Tilly and I are parked in front. We are going to walk around the side of the house and distract the douchebag still waiting on your front porch."

"See you later, Willow!" Tilly sent her a grin before following Arabella outside into the darkness.

"We'll go around the other side of the house," Calla said, slipping outside, with the others following her.

"Seriously," Willow murmured, looking around in confusion, "what just happened?"

"We are saving you from the man out front," Desi teased, catching her hand and dragging her out the door, then making sure it was locked behind them.

"But…"

"Shhh," Desi whispered, putting her gloved finger up to her lips. "We need to hurry. He's already looking for you."

Willow realized in surprise that her friend was right. The distraction of her coven didn't seem to be working. Derek was asking rather loudly where she was.

"What is wrong with him?" It didn't make sense. Derek had flirted hardcore with her in the past, but always moved on when she shot him down. This was something altogether different, bordering on stalker material. If she was honest, it was starting to freak her out.

"I have no idea, but let's get the hell out of here."

Willow followed Desi through her back yard, realizing too late that her white coat had been a bad idea. It stood out brightly in the darkness. Derek rounded the side of the house just as they reached her back gate.

"Willow, please, just listen to me."

"Look, Derek, I have no idea what's going on here, but I've already told you how I feel."

"I just want a chance," he said imploringly, making his way through a small snowdrift as he came up to her fence. "I think we could do great things together."

"Not a chance, buddy," Desi cut in, tugging Willow through the back gate. "Willow already has someone to do great things with." With a slight wave of her hand, she stopped Derek in his tracks long enough for them to make it to her car and slide quickly inside.

"I can't believe you just did that," Willow groused, putting her seatbelt on, before glancing through the back window and waving her own hand to undo the spell.

"That guy was starting to get on my nerves."

"That guy is one of my bosses."

"The dirty one who is always trying to get in your pants."

"Yeah, but…"

"But what?" Desi asked, glancing over at her.

"This was just… off."

"Off how?"

"I don't know. I mean, he's always been a slimeball, but right now I feel…"

"Violated?" Desi asked quietly.

"Yeah." Willow glanced down at her hands before looking over at her friend. "He came to my home, Desi."

"Your sanctuary."

"After I just told him in no uncertain terms that there was not now, nor would there ever be, anything between us."

Desi was silent for a moment before she said, "I think you need to talk to someone about this, Willow."

"Like who?"

"I don't know. The police?"

Willow shook her head. "No, there isn't anything they can do about it. He hasn't done anything illegal."

"Well, file a restraining order against the bastard."

"Kind of hard to do when he's my boss," Willow muttered, a short laugh escaping; although no part of her felt like laughing right now.

"Willow, this is serious. I got a very fucked up vibe from that guy."

Willow sighed, leaning her head back against the car seat. If she was honest with herself, she'd been getting bad vibes from Derek for over a year now, but she shrugged it off. She had one goal at Johnson and Johnson, and that was making partner. She was so close; she could taste it.

"I really think you need to tell someone about this," Desi insisted. "Whether it be the police or someone higher up than him at your company. It needs to stop."

She was right. Everything Desi was saying, Willow had already thought. It was following through with the action that was bothering her.

"It's not as easy as you would think, Desi. You don't understand."

"So, explain it to me."

Desi turned down the street that would take them into the business district of their city, and Willow realized she had no idea where they were going. Not that it mattered. The end result was going to be her, in the same room with Dominic Hamilton. If anything, it would ease the ache in her chest slightly so she could focus, and possibly figure out what to do about her current situation with her douchebag stalker.

"Derek Johnson is the grandson of Henry Johnson, the owner of Johnson and Johnson Law Firm."

"Well, shit."

"Yeah, and it gets worse."

"Can't get much worse than that."

"His father was the other owner of the company. He died a few years ago, right after they brough Derek on.

Since then, Henry has been grooming Derek to take over the company when he retires in a couple of years."

"Wait, a minute. Exactly how old is Derek? Because the man I just saw looked like he had to at least be in his late thirties."

"He's forty-two."

"So, that would make his grandfather how old?"

"Henry is eighty-three. I think he would have retired already, except Derek is a little…" Willow paused, searching for the right word.

"He's an egotistical asshat who isn't yet capable of running a law firm."

"That pretty much sums it up."

Desi pulled into the parking lot at Club Nightlife, cutting the engine before turning to look at Willow. "Why haven't you told me any of this before? I mean, you told me a little bit about Derek, but not exactly who he was, or how much he scares you."

Willow could hear the hurt in Desi's voice, and knew she'd messed up not sharing more with her friend, but that just wasn't the kind of person she was. She tended to keep most things to herself, not wanting to involve anyone else in her problems. "It really wasn't that bad until recently," she hedged. And, for the most part, it was the truth.

"Still, you should have said something."

"You're right. I'm sorry."

Desi was quiet for a moment, then reached over to cover Willow's hand with hers. "It doesn't matter. The main thing is that you told me now."

For the first time in years, Willow felt tears prick the back of her eyes as she whispered, "Thank you."

"Just one thing, Willow."

"Yeah?"

"If you refuse to tell anyone, there is only one thing we can do."

Willow's eyes narrowed on Desi, knowing she shouldn't ask, but couldn't help herself. "What's that?"

"Call the coven in, of course. Were gonna light that freaky bastard on fire. It will teach him to mess with one of us."

"Desi!"

"Or," Desi said, opening her door, "we can turn him into a drooling zombie. That could be fun."

"Desi, seriously!"

Desi met her gaze steadily, her brown eyes taking on a golden, glowing tint. "I am serious, Willow. No one fucks with my sister."

Willow felt the woman's vow deep in her soul. Desi was going to be the High Priestess of the Sapphire Coven someday, there was no doubt in her mind. And she would always protect them, no matter the cost.

CHAPTER FOUR

"What are we doing here, Drake?"

It wasn't the first time Dominic had asked the question, and he was still waiting impatiently for an answer. He'd finally woken up just a couple of hours ago from the long ass catnap his grandmother had put him in. Before he knew what was happening, his brother had shoved him into the shower, waited until he put on some clothes, and then dragged him out of the house and down to the bar. It had been months since he'd been to a bar, and he had no desire to be there now.

"Meeting Desi and Willow for drinks."

Dominic slowly put the tumbler of whiskey he was holding down in front of him, leaned forward, placing his forearms on the table and growled, "You mind repeating yourself, Brother?"

"You heard me."

"Just the four of us?"

"Yes."

"Why?"

"Because you are too bullheaded to pick up the phone and call the woman, you can't stop thinking about. You need her."

He was right, and Dominic knew it. He'd fought against it for so long, but not only did he want Willow, he did need her. Still, that didn't make it right. "She could do better."

"Yeah, well, she doesn't get a choice in the matter anymore and neither do you."

"She deserves one," Dominic argued. "You were looking for one for Desi. You could find one for Willow so she has a choice."

"It wouldn't do any good if I tried," Drake said, leaning in closer to him. "But, I won't."

"Dammit, why not?"

Drake reached over and laid a hand on his wrist, giving it a squeeze. "Because, Dom, you *do* deserve this, whether you think you do or not. You deserve happiness. To find that person who completes you. Someone to love you, someone to love back. The Goddess has placed her in front of you, and I refuse to sit back and watch you ruin it."

Dominic swallowed hard, dropping his gaze to the table. "What if I can't do this?"

Drake's eyes darkened in anger as he ground out, "Would you prefer to live half a life? To force Willow to live half a life? To constantly be in pain, silently suffering on the inside, knowing she's out there somewhere without you going through the same thing?"

Well, when he put it that way. "No."

"Then pull your head out of your ass, Brother. Man up and claim what is yours."

"What are you two boys talking about? I could feel the tension the moment we walked in the room."

Desi's voice pulled Dominic's attention away from his brother, and over to where she stood next to his Willow. His. It sounded right, no matter how much he fought it. And he was so tired of fighting.

Her hair flowed over her shoulders in blue waves, standing out brightly against the pure white coat she wore. Her dark green eyes were full of shadows, and there were small worry lines on her brow that weren't there before. *Had he put them there?*

"Nothing," Drake said, sliding an arm around Desi's waist and scooting back away from the table enough so he could pull her down on his lap. "Just brother stuff."

As Dominic watched, Willow glanced around the bar warily, before slipping out of her coat and placing it over the chair directly across from him. He found he didn't want her to be so far away. Reaching over, he slid the chair closer to him out. His hand on the back of it, he met her gaze and nodded to it. He saw the flicker of surprise in her eyes before a cool mask covered her features, but she did move her coat over and slowly sat down on the chair.

"So, we had an interesting night," Desi sang out, before taking her husband's glass from him and taking a sip. Making a face, she sputtered, "Water? We're at a bar, and you're drinking water?"

He grinned. "Designated driver."

Dominic watched them but kept most of his attention on Willow. Something was wrong with her. She'd been unable to hide the flinch when Desi said something about their night, but the expression on her face never changed. It was as if it were carved from granite.

"Tell us about your night," Drake prompted, kissing Desi's temple before looking over at Willow and giving her a grin. "I heard popcorn and movies were on the list."

"And Willow's lovely stalker, who topped the list when he showed up in the middle of the movie," Desi said, her hand going out to snag Dominic's whiskey from the table.

He let her have it, his focus completely on Willow now; his protective instincts rising. "What stalker?"

"It's nothing," Willow snapped, turning those flashing green eyes on Desi. "Everything's fine."

"No, it isn't, Willow. If you want my opinion, the man is deranged. The vibes he was giving off made my skin crawl."

Dominic could tell Willow was pissed that Desi had brought it up, but he wasn't letting it go now. He may have been fighting his attraction to the beautiful woman in front of him, the pull between them that was both magical and real, but he wasn't going to sit back while she was in danger.

"Talk to us, Willow. Let us help."

She pulled her gaze from Desi to look at him, and he felt his heart literally jump in his chest when their eyes met. There was a tightening—a squeezing sensation, different from the painful aching one he'd had over the past couple of months. It was as if something inside of him was reaching for something inside of her. He knew from what Drake and Desi had gone through that it was their magic, but he'd never experienced anything like it before. Not this strong, almost irresistible link that seemed to be tightening between them.

"Desi is blowing it all out of proportion," Willow finally said, lowering her gaze to the table.

"Are you scared?" When she didn't answer, he reached over and cupped her chin in his hand, gently tilting her head up until their eyes met once again. "Are you scared of this man, Willow?"

She bit her lip, and he nearly groaned out loud. He wanted to do that. Trace those full red lips with his tongue, nibble on them, taste them. He had to remind himself that now was not the time.

"I wasn't."

"But?"

"He showed up at my home, Dominic."

In all the time they'd known each other, the times they'd been at the same gatherings with Drake and Desi, never once had she said his name. His heart clenched at the vulnerability in her eyes and the fear in her voice. Willow was a strong, powerful, capable woman. He'd seen her in action and knew she could hold her own. It would take a lot to scare her.

"Uninvited," Desi cut in.

"I've never had anyone there before except my sisters. No one. I like my privacy."

"How did he get your address?"

He was aware that Drake and Desi were watching the exchange with interest, but he ignored them. Willow was his only concern right now.

"Technically, he's one of my bosses. The owner's grandson. So, he would have access to the records at work. I've never personally given anyone there my address except the human resources department."

"That's a violation of your privacy," he growled. "I don't give a damn who he is."

Tears filled her eyes, and she lowered her lids, trying to

hide them from view. "He's probably harmless, but after tonight, I just don't know."

"He's not harmless, Willow," Desi interjected. "He's dangerous. I don't like the thought of you going home alone tonight. I think you better come stay with us."

"No," Willow protested, yanking her chin from his hand and glaring over at Desi. "I won't let that bastard push me out of my own house."

"You can't stay there alone," Desi argued. "It isn't safe."

"She won't be alone." When all eyes turned toward him, Dominic covered Willow's hand with his. "I'm not leaving her until we get this figured out."

"And after that?" Willow asked, her voice so low he almost didn't hear her over the din of the music in the background.

Unsure what she really wanted, he asked, "How about we play it one day at a time?"

Willow nodded slowly, before turning her hand over and lacing their fingers together. "One day at a time."

CHAPTER FIVE

"Nice neighborhood," Dominic said quietly, as he followed her directions and turned down the street her house was on.

"Yeah," she whispered, exhaustion beating at her.

"Good neighbors?"

Were they really going to have a mundane conversation about where she lived when there were so many more interesting things they could be discussing right now?

"As far as I know. I haven't met any of them, but I haven't had any issues."

"Did you just move in?"

Willow frowned, turning to look at him. "No, I've lived here for a couple of years now. Why?"

Dominic glanced over at her in surprise. "You've lived here for two years and have no idea who your neighbors are?"

His eyes were an electric blue, and so captivating Willow almost let him drive by her house. "Wait, turn here!" When he slowed down and pulled into her driveway, she whispered softly under her breath, raising a hand and flicking her wrist, watching as her garage door began to open. "Park on the left side."

The second they were inside, she lowered the door back down, praying Derek wasn't out there somewhere watching. The thought of it pissed her off on many different levels. She was angry that the son of a bitch was acting so crazy, but even more angry that she was letting him frighten her. She was in her thirties and had stopped being afraid of things that went bump in the night years ago. She was not going to let this poor excuse of a man ruin her life. But she also wasn't willing to give up Dominic's reassuring presence at the time, either.

"You haven't gone to any street parties? No barbeques? Nothing?"

"What the hell are you talking about?" Street parties? Did people even have those anymore?

"You said you haven't met any of your neighbors. I find it really hard to believe that you've lived here as long as you have, and you don't know any of them."

"Believe what you want," she snapped, reaching for the doorhandle next to her. She froze when she felt Dominic's hand on her arm. It was a gentle touch, one that she felt through the layers of her thick coat and long-sleeved shirt. One she wanted to lean in to.

"Hey, I didn't mean anything by it."

Looking over at him, Willow sucked in a short breath. His blue eyes were filled with a compassion she didn't deserve, along with something else. Something she wasn't ready to acknowledge. When her tongue slipped out to wet her suddenly dry lips, those eyes dropped to her mouth. His hand tightened slightly, and a low groan filled the air.

When he raised his gaze to meet hers again, his eyes had darkened and were swirling with emotion.

Suddenly, the car seemed too small. The air around them was thick and so damn hot. She felt her magic come forth, as if it was searching for his, and the feeling was as exciting as it was scary.

"Willow." Her name was a deep groan on his lips, and it sent a ripple of desire through her. Her nipples hardened, her breath coming out in small pants.

Dominic's hand came up to delve in her hair, cupping the back of her head and pulling her closer, his mouth hovering right over hers. Willow's heart began to race, and that invisible thread that seemed to run between the two of them pulled tight.

"Dominic, please."

"Fuck, baby, if you don't want this, you better walk away right now."

The air around them crackled with electricity, their magic colliding as Willow closed the distance between them and placed her lips on his. There was no turning back. She wanted him, needed him, and she was going to have him.

Dominic took over, his mouth hard and heavy on hers. Devouring, taking, demanding. His tongue pushed past her lips, tangling with hers. She heard a zipper being lowered, and then his hand was inside her coat, stroking over her stomach, and sliding up under her shirt.

Willow moaned when he found her breast, his thumb sliding up under the thin, lacy material to knead it gently before pinching her beaded nipple lightly. She cried out, feeling as if she was on fire, flames that only Dominic could put out.

Dominic's mouth left hers to place hot, wet kisses over her jawline and down her neck. He stopped at the place where her pulse was beating wildly, stroking his tongue over her skin, and then sucking gently.

Willow's hands went to his nice, black dress shirt. She began to undo the buttons, one-by-one, itching to touch the chest with a light smattering of hair she was revealing. "So sexy," she murmured, sliding her fingers into the hair and tugging gently.

The next thing she knew, his hands were on her hips and he was lifting her from her seat over to his, placing her knees on both sides of his legs so she was straddling him. Then, his mouth was back, that tongue licking, his mouth sucking, driving her insane.

His cock was hard and thick, pressing up into the now damp material that covered her wet pussy. She shuddered at the way he felt, wishing nothing separated them. She clutched the lapels of his shirt tightly, yanking them apart, making the rest of the buttons fly as she bared his full chest and stomach to her hungry view. So fucking sexy.

"Damn woman," Dominic growled as he arched up into her. "You losing control is the hottest thing I've ever seen."

Willow couldn't respond. She was beyond words. She shivered, tremors running over her body as she felt her magic flowing around them, merging in the air with Dominic's. She'd never seen or felt anything like it.

"I need to be inside you," Dominic rasped, his mouth finding hers once again. Willow felt him slide the front of her shirt down, moving her bra to the side, baring her breast to him. Cupping it, he leaned forward and closed his mouth over her nipple, sucking hard and then biting down gently, before sucking again. Willow threw her head back and called his name as she felt the beginning of an orgasm rising in her. She began to rotate her hips, rocking against his hard cock, moaning as she chased her climax. She was so close.

Suddenly, she felt Dominic's hand move over her hip to her belly, and then slip inside the waistband of her pants. His fingers skimmed lower, over her damp folds, and then two of them slid inside.

"Oh Goddess!" she cried, grasping his shoulders tightly, digging her nails into his skin.

Dominic's thumb found her clit, and he flicked it once, twice, and then began to rub against it, causing hot flames to shoot through her. Unable to stop herself, Willow lifted her hips up and down, riding those magical fingers.

"Come for me," Dominic demanded, right before he bit down on her nipple, just a little harder than he had before.

Willow screamed as she flew apart, coating his hand with her cream. Dominic found her mouth with his, muffling her cries as she continued his onslaught, rubbing her clit and pushing his fingers in and out of her. Soon, she was going over the edge again, falling apart in his arms. She'd never come so hard before, never felt anything like what she felt in Dominic's arms.

Fully sated, she laid her head on his shoulder. The events of the day had caught up with her, and even though she fought against it, she was unable to keep her eyes open. "Sorry," she whispered, snuggling into him.

"For what?"

She heard the confusion in his voice and tried to explain. "You didn't get to finish."

Dominic chuckled softly, placing a kiss on her temple. "You did. That's all that matters."

"No." She wanted to argue with him. To tell him he was important too. But she couldn't seem to form a coherent sentence.

"You are the only thing that matters," he said quietly.

She was unaware when he opened the door and slid out of the vehicle, gathering her in his arms and carrying her into the house. Leaving the lights off, he made his way through the kitchen, finding the stairs that would take them up to her room. After placing her on her bed, he slid off her coat that was still clinging to her lower arms, and then her boots. Tucking her in, he placed a kiss on her forehead. When she moaned, a small frown appeared on her face as she muttered his name. Dominic kicked off his shoes, removed his shirt, and slid into bed beside her, pulling her close.

"Sleep, Willow. I'm here now. You're safe."

CHAPTER SIX

Dominic opened his eyes the next morning to the smell of bacon and an empty bed. The first was welcome, the second was not. He'd spent the majority of the night holding Willow close to him, ignoring the fact that he was hard as a fucking rock, knowing there was a very real chance when they awoke that his woman would run. She was a contradiction; one he was hoping to unravel.

From what he could tell, she was close to her coven sisters, but they were her only family. Not only that, but they were the only ones she let near her. She had co-workers, but no other friends or acquaintances that she interacted with. Hell, she didn't even seem to know who her neighbors were. She'd admitted the night before that she had never actually met any of them.

Frowning, he pushed down the covers and slid from the bed. He wondered where he fit into the equation. Just because the Goddess paired them together for eternity, didn't mean Willow would accept it, or him. The problem was, they couldn't just walk away from each other. Once the Goddess made her choice, you were stuck.

Dominic slowly pulled the covers up, placing the pillows over the comforter as he contemplated his next course of action. He had two choices. He could walk away from Willow once he made sure her stalker situation was under control and live a half-life without her. That was what he'd planned to do since the moment he found out what it meant when their magic reached for each other. When he thought he didn't deserve someone like Willow. Hell, he still thought that. Or, he could man up and fight like hell to keep the gift the Goddess had given him.

He paused in the act of fixing the comforter so that it fell on each side of the bed equally. The Goddess had gifted him with the chance to spend eternity with the woman downstairs. Strong, beautiful, courageous Willow. That meant even if *he* didn't believe he was worthy, Fate did.

Unsure what to think about that, Dominic walked into Willow's bathroom to use the facilities, then used the unopened toothbrush he found on the counter by the sink.

The biggest question was, what was he going to do? Dominic sighed, turning to leave the room. There was only one answer.

There was no way he was going to just let her go. He couldn't. He was going to fight for what was his.

After ascending the stairs, he wandered through Willow's home to the kitchen, taking more time this morning to look around. It was decent sized, clean, and not at all what he would have pictured for Willow. The rooms were decorated in bright pastel colors, where he would have pictured more reds, oranges, and yellows to match her fiery disposition. The pastels hinted at a softer side, one he found that he really wanted to know.

Dominic smiled when he saw Willow leaning up against the island in the kitchen, crunching on a piece of overcooked bacon while talking on her phone. She was dressed in black yoga pants with a bright pink T-shirt that hugged her body in all the right places. Pink, not the normal black, brown, or gray he was used to seeing her in. The colors a prominent, dressed-to-impress attorney would wear. He was seeing a different side of his Willow today and loving it so far.

"I'll be there."

Dominic tuned in to the conversation when he heard those words, wondering where they were going. Because he wasn't letting Willow out of his sight until the fool who thought he could put the look of fear on her face, that he did the night before, was taken care of. One way or another.

"I'll ask him."

Him?

Willow glanced his way, giving him a small smile. "Dom's a big boy. If he wants to come, he can."

Just those words alone had Dominic's dick hardening almost to the point of pain. She was right on both counts.

Something in his eyes must have told her where his thoughts had gone, because her gaze left his and slowly tracked down his body, stopping where his aching cock now tented his pants. She licked her lips, those green eyes darkening to a deep emerald color.

"I'm going to have to let you go."

The breathless tone in her voice had him moving toward her, his eyes glued to where that pretty pink tongue was peeking out between her full, pouty lips. He knew where he wanted those lips.

"Hang up the phone, Willow," he ordered, his hands going to the belt at his waist. He'd been denied what he really wanted last night. He didn't want to wait any longer. And judging by how quickly she got rid of whoever was on the other line before tossing her cell on the island, she didn't either.

Reaching out, Willow knocked his hands away from his belt, grasping it herself and quickly undoing and removing it. The button on his pants and zipper were next. They were in a pool at his feet, along with his boxer briefs, before he knew it.

"I love it when you take charge, baby," he growled. "It turns me the fuck on."

Her eyes met his as she grasped her shirt by the hem and pulled it up and over her head. "Good, 'cause I'm a take charge kind of woman."

"My kind of woman," he rasped, watching as she slowly lowered herself to her knees before him.

A shudder ran through him when Willow reached out and trailed her hands over his stomach, down his hips, and around to his ass. Leaning forward, placing her lips over the head of his cock, her eyes locked with his as she slowly pushed down, engulfing him in the hot cavern of her mouth. He groaned her name, a hand sliding into her thick hair as he watched her begin to move. She took as much of him as she could, and then paused, before sliding back up his length. Sucking gently on the tip of his straining erection, she moaned in pleasure. That one sound almost sent him over the edge.

The sight of those bright red lips sliding over his dick had him pushing into her mouth again, unable to stop himself. He was aware of the electricity flowing through the air. Their magic intertwining, like a hot, wild current of energy, making the hair on his arms stand on end. The lights began to flicker out of control, matching the way he was feeling.

Dominic felt the thread that had begun to tie him and Willow together months ago, begin to pull tighter than it ever had before, and he almost jumped when one of the bulbs in the light over the kitchen table popped. He moved to pull out of Willow's hot, enticing mouth, but she tightened her hold on his ass, digging her nails in.

"I want to be inside you, Willow," he rasped, a need that couldn't be ignored. As much as he loved the things she was currently doing to him with her mouth and tongue, he wanted something else even more.

Reluctantly, she let him pull out of her mouth, and then help her to her feet. "Bedroom?"

Dominic shook his head. "Too far away." His hands slid into the top of those ass hugging yoga pants, sliding them down and off her. The hot pink thong followed, and then the matching bra. Soon, he had her naked before him, his eyes raking over her body and taking in her every curve.

Sliding his hands under her bottom, he lifted her, biting back a groan when her wet pussy slid over the length of his cock. Willow's hands came up to clutch at his shoulders, and he slowly lowered her down on his dick, cursing when he was enclosed in walls of heat. Gritting his teeth tightly, he fought back the urge to come right then.

"Dominic!"

"Fuck, Willow," he muttered, walking forward until her back hit the wall.

"I wish you would!" she snapped, her green eyes flashing at him.

She didn't have to tell him twice. Slamming his mouth down on hers, Dominic began to move. Pushing in and out of her in quick, fast thrusts, he claimed her mouth as he claimed the rest of her body. It was his, all of it, and he knew at that moment that he would never be able to let her go.

His magic surged forward, powerful and commanding. Willow's met his halfway. It began to swarm around them, in them, merging until there was no Dominic's magic and Willow's magic. Now, you couldn't tell them apart.

Willow laid her head back against the wall, clutching his shoulders tightly, her nails digging in so deep he knew she would leave marks. He didn't care. Let her mark him. Claim him like he was hers. They belonged with one another. Together for eternity.

Dominic's hips pistoned back and forth, his cock driving in and out of Willow's wet heat. Cupboard doors began to open and then slam shut. The coffee cup Willow had left on the island jumped around until it fell to the floor and broke. The pictures on the walls moved back and forth, a couple slipping off the nails they were hanging on and crashing to the floor.

Willow stiffened, screaming his name, and then shattered around him, squeezing his shaft tightly and wringing his own orgasm from him. He shouted, slamming into her one last time, before he came deep inside her, giving her everything he had—everything he was.

Breathing heavily, Dominic slowly lowered Willow to the floor, holding her close to him while he gently stroked her hair. He felt his magic return to him, but it was different. It wasn't just *his* anymore. It was a combination of his and hers. It felt different… and right.

CHAPTER SEVEN

"So, you want me to go with you where?"

Willow laughed as she swept up the last of the broken glass on the floor and dumped it into the trash can. After putting the broom away, she turned back to look at the man who was quickly capturing her heart. He was repositioning one of her pictures on the wall, now dressed in a dark blue pullover and a pair of jeans that gently cupped his firm ass that he'd had in a duffle bag in his car.

Thoughts of the shower they'd just shared came to mind, and she had to stop herself from crossing the room to jump him again. Her damn lady parts were tingling, and she wanted to run her hands over the curve of his round…

"Willow?"

Willow slowly brought her eyes up from his ass to meet his gaze, just then realizing he was glancing over his shoulder at her with a smirk on his face.

"What?"

"Where are we going?"

"Oh! Desi and Drake want us to meet them at Desi's

grandmother's to help them decorate that huge tree in front of Farrah's house. It's something they do every year."

"Do you normally go?"

Willow shrugged, crossing her arms over her chest. "No. Usually, I'm working."

Dominic nodded, stepping back to give the picture one last look before turning to face her. "And here?"

Willow cocked an eyebrow. "What do you mean?"

"Do you decorate here for Christmas?"

She shook her head. "It doesn't make sense. I'm hardly ever here to enjoy it."

Dominic frowned, his eyes going beyond her to the hallway and what he could see of the living room. "Did you decorate your house, Willow, or hire a contractor?"

Willow blushed, following his gaze. "I did. When I'm home, I like to be surrounded by things that make me happy."

Dominic was quiet for a moment before he slowly crossed the room toward her. Taking her hands in his, he tugged her to him, leaning down to place a gentle kiss on her lips. "So, which one of your personas are the real you?"

"I have more than one?"

Chuckling, he nodded. "There's the strong, sassy female who makes me want to pull my hair out one minute and kiss her senseless the next. The no-nonsense attorney who only wears blacks, browns, and gray tones, who makes me want to bend her over a desk and fuck her senseless. And then there's this Willow." He waved around the kitchen and living room areas. "The one who embraces her softer side. Shows her heart just a little bit more. The one I want to love senseless."

Willow stiffened, ducking her head, knowing her face was bright red with embarrassment now. One moment Dominic made her feel all hot and bothered, the next vulnerable and nervous.

"Tell me why you don't like to let people close, Willow." Willow tried to pull away, but Dominic wouldn't let her. "Baby, please, talk to me."

Willow fought back the tears that threatened, not wanting to show him how much his question hurt. She did let people close. Well, one person. Desi.

"Why don't you know anything about your neighbors after living here for over two years? Why don't you have any friends except for your coven sisters? You have to know people from work? But you keep them at a distance, too?"

"Dominic, stop!" Willow demanded, yanking out of his arms, and taking several steps down the hall away from him. "Just stop!"

Dominic's eyes clouded over, and he hung his head for a moment. Then he raised it and met hers. "Let me tell you why I do it, and then maybe, someday, you will share it with me."

What? She'd never noticed Dominic keeping his distance from others. Exactly the opposite, actually. He was always talking, laughing, and teasing people. Willow frowned. That was right. The more she thought about it, the more she realized that it was all superficial. It was only with his brother and Desi, and sometimes her. When her coven sisters were around, he was polite, but more guarded. Why hadn't she noticed that before?

"I fell in love when I was a teenager," Dominic started. "Unfortunately, it was with my best friend's girl, who was also one of my best friends." Sighing, he turned and walked into the living room to stare out the front window. Placing his hands on his hips, he continued. "She was everything I thought I wanted at the time. Beautiful. Long, blonde hair. Big blue eyes. Sweet and innocent. A big, caring heart."

"She sounds great," Willow said softly, wondering where this story was going.

"She was," Dominic agreed. "Her name was Sydney. She and her family moved to town when I was a junior in high school. From the moment I saw her, I only had eyes for her, but she only had eyes for Brandon."

"That's how it goes sometimes," Willow murmured. "You can't choose who you fall in love with."

Dominic glanced back at her and nodded, before looking out the window again. "True, but you can choose whether or not you act on it. I chose incorrectly."

"What do you mean?"

Dominic inhaled deeply before turning to face her. His eyes were dark and tumultuous, full of sorrow and regret. It took everything inside her not to go to him and wrap her arms around him tightly.

"We were at a party one night. A huge bonfire with a bunch of underage kids drinking, laughing, and having a good time. I cornered Sydney out by the barn while Brandon was inside getting some more beer. I was drunk, so was she." Dominic swallowed hard, raking a hand through his hair. "I made the mistake of telling her how I felt and tried to kiss her."

"I take it that didn't go over so well?"

"Naw." He shook his head. "She smacked me so hard it smacked me sober. Made me realized what a fool I was being. But, by then it was too late. Brandon showed up, and she told him what happened. He told me what a shitty friend I was, and he wasn't wrong."

Willow took a step toward him, unable to stop herself. "What happened, Dom?"

Dominic's jaw tightened—hard as granite. Then he muttered, "They left. Brandon was pissed. He'd been drinking. He lost control of his car." Dominic reached up and swiped at his eyes, trying to hide the moisture that appeared. "They didn't make it."

Willow crossed the room and slid her arms around his waist, pulling him close. Resting her head on his chest, she held him tightly to her. "That wasn't your fault, Dom."

"I hit on his girl."

Willow leaned back to look at him. "Who the fuck cares?"

"What?"

Willow saw the shock on his face, but she ignored it. He obviously needed a wake-up call if he'd spent his entire life blaming his friends' death on himself. "They both made the decision to drink. He made the decision to drive. She made the decision to get in the car." Sliding her hands up, she cupped his cheeks. "Dom, all you did was tell someone that you cared about them. While it might not have been the best thing to do, you did not make them get into that car. That's on them."

"They *died!*"

"Yes, and it sucks. It really fucking sucks. But it *isn't* your fault, Dom." Rising up on her toes, she kissed his mouth softly. "It isn't your fault."

A shudder racked Dominic's body, and then he pulled her close, burying his face in her neck. Willow felt his tears on her skin as he rasped, "I hated myself for so long. I believed I didn't deserve to find love because I ruined theirs. That I didn't deserve you, even though the Goddess thought I did for some reason."

"You should probably change your thinking from being worried you don't deserve me to being worried that you are stuck with me," Willow teased. "Because, from what Desi tells me, once what we did this morning happens, there is no going back."

Dominic raised his head, meeting her eyes. "I don't want to go back, Willow Ryder."

CHAPTER EIGHT

Dominic stood off to the side of the huge tree, his heart feeling lighter than it had for as long as he could remember as he watched Willow with her coven sisters. He'd never shared what happened that night with anyone except his brother. Not even his grandmother knew the full story. The guilt and shame that had been his constant companion for so many years wasn't entirely gone, but it had lessened tremendously.

Willow made him feel things he had never felt before. Hell, he'd never even made it beyond a third date in the past, unwilling to string anyone along knowing he had nothing to offer them. With Willow, it was different. He wanted to give her everything.

"Love's a powerful thing, isn't it, brother?"

Dominic tore his gaze away from the woman who represented his future to glance over at Drake. "Yeah, it is."

"You tell her how you feel?"

Dominic slowly shook his head. "Not yet."

Drake clapped a hand on his shoulder, squeezing it gently. "Don't wait too long."

"Drake, you and Dominic need to come put the star on top!" Desi hollered.

Staring at the two ladders that ran almost to the top of the tree on either side of it, Dominic raised an eyebrow. "We just spent an hour stringing lights around that mammoth thing, and now they want us back up at the top of it? Why didn't they have us do it earlier when we were already up there?"

Drake shrugged, grinning at him. "Because they are evil witches and like to see us sweat."

"Can't we just float the thing up there?"

Chuckling, Drake began to walk away. "Don't worry, Dom. I've got your back. I won't let them know how scared of heights you are."

Dominic groaned loudly when all eyes turned his way. He was going to kill his brother later. Unfortunately, what Drake said was the truth. He may have hung the lights without comment, but he'd been nervous as hell the entire time, and no part of him wanted to go back up there again.

Before he could reply, Willow was beside him, sliding her arm through his, and giving him one of her amazing smiles. "I think we've helped enough for the night. What do you say we go home and watch a movie?"

"You can't leave yet," Desi protested. "It's only five o'clock. We can't even light the tree until at least seven."

"There is no way I'm staying here a couple more hours," Willow muttered, her grip on Dominic's arm tightening. "We're going to have to make a run for it."

Dominic threw his head back and laughed, unable to stop himself. He knew she was trying to deflect the attention from him and his fear, and he couldn't have loved her more than he did at that moment.

Cupping her cheek in his gloved hand, he leaned down and kissed her lips softly. "Thank you, baby."

"For what?" she asked, giving him an innocent look. Then, she ruined it by pursing her lips, blowing him a kiss, and giving him a sassy wink.

Shaking his head, Dominic pulled away from her and walked over to the same ladder he was on earlier. The star was huge, and there was no way his brother was going to be able to hang it by himself. Grasping a rope that one of Willow's sisters handed him, Calla if he remembered correctly, he began to climb slowly. Drake was on the other side, clutching tightly to a separate rope as he made his way up his ladder.

Dominic was halfway up when he froze, a feeling of unease pushing at him that had nothing to do with his fear of heights. Frowning, he looked down at the others below, trying to see if any of them sensed anything.

Farrah was standing off to the side talking to her best friends, Glenda and Salena. Two of Willow's sisters who were married were a little further away with their husbands and children building a snowman. Desi was with her sister and cousin, laughing about something. Willow was waiting patiently where he'd left her, but she took a step in his direction when their eyes met.

"Dominic, you okay over there? You need me to shoulder your part, too?" Drake teased loudly.

Ignoring him, Dominic let his gaze travel beyond

Willow. Farrah lived in a large house in a nice neighborhood, where all the homes were spaced approximately half a mile apart. She was on a corner lot, and all of their vehicles were in her long driveway. There was only one car nearby that wasn't. A dark, four-door sedan that was parked halfway down the street. Not in front of any house. It looked vacant, but something about it bothered him. It didn't make sense that it was sitting where it was. It would have been a long walk to any house. So why was it there?

Dominic had just reached out with his magic, trying to decipher exactly what it was that had him so on edge, when a loud crack sounded around them, and then something slammed into his chest, jerking him from the ladder and sending him sailing through the air. He heard Willow cry out and several of the other women scream as he fell to the ground, aware of magic being used to cushion his fall as he landed on the snow below. A muffled curse left his mouth at the searing pain close to his heart, but he shoved it aside as he tried to rise to his feet.

"Dom! Fuck, Dom!"

Suddenly, Drake was by his side, holding him down. Vaguely, he wondered how his brother had gotten there so fast. The second the thought crossed his mind; he knew the answer. Magic. Then, he was aware of Willow next to him, tears streaming down her face as she grasped his hand and pushed a lock of hair from his forehead.

"Sniper," Dominic managed to spit out roughly, as he tried to sit up again. His vision wavered, dizziness swamping him, and he had to fight not to pass out. It was the only thing that made sense. Whoever drove that car was hiding somewhere with a rifle that could be trained on them right now.

"What?"

"Sniper. Down the street," Dominic gasped, dropping back down against the snow. No matter how hard he tried, he couldn't sit up. "Got to keep Willow safe."

"I'm safe, Dom," Willow whispered, leaning over to place her cheek against his. "I'm right here, with you."

"I've got you, Brother. I have a force-field up around us so tight right now, nothing can penetrate it."

Dominic was once again trying to rise to protect his witch, and the confidence in his brother's voice was the only thing that made him back down. Drake would make sure Willow was safe when he couldn't. He didn't know of many warlocks stronger than his brother.

"Willow," Dominic gasped her name as he struggled to breathe. It felt as if a huge weight was sitting on his chest, crushing him. He knew he was fighting a losing battle. "Baby."

"I'm right here, Dom."

Her breath was on his face, her tears falling from her cheeks to his own.

"Don't you dare leave me, Dominic Hamilton. Not now. Not after I just found you."

He didn't want to leave her. Didn't want to be anywhere but by her side. He tried to tell her that. He opened his mouth, but no words came out.

"Should we try to use our magic," he heard a timid voice ask. Tilly maybe? "Maybe we could get the bullet out of him."

"We can't. At this point, it could do more harm than good. We are going to have to wait for the doctors to handle it." That was Farrah, the High Priestess of the Sapphire Coven.

"There has to be something we can do," someone else said. There were other voices chiming in, but everything was getting all muddled together now. He couldn't concentrate, couldn't focus on anything.

"The ambulance is almost here, Brother. I hear the sirens. I'm letting the force field down so they can get in. Don't worry, there's no way that bastard stuck around for the after party."

Dominic heard what Drake was saying, but it was as if the words were coming to him through a long tunnel and far away. He fought to get back to his brother, back to Willow and the love he'd just found with her. He needed to tell her how he felt. She needed to know that she was his life—his everything.

"Dammit, Dom, don't do this!" Willow cried. "Please! You can't leave me like everyone else. Please, come back to me!"

Like everyone else? Who'd left his Willow? Who had hurt her?

"You need to move aside, Ma'am."

"No!"

Dominic felt her grasp on him tighten, and he tried to pry his eyes open. To tell her he was all right. That he loved her and would never leave her.

"Ma'am, we can't do our job with you on top of him like that."

"Willow, come on. Let them work."

Dominic heard his sister-in-law trying to coax Willow away, and then he heard Willow whisper for his ears alone, "You come back to me. You hear me, Dominic Hamilton? You fight like you've never fought before. If you go, you take my heart and soul with you, and I will follow. So, fight, dammit! Fight!"

That was the last thing he heard before everything went dark.

CHAPTER NINE

Terror gripped her as Willow sat in the waiting room at the hospital, clutching Desi's hand tightly. After the ambulance left with Dominic, the rest of them had to stay behind to give statements to the police. There wasn't much they could tell them, except about Willow's creepy co-worker, but as far as she knew, Derek didn't have any experience with weapons. By the time they got to the hospital, Dominic was already in surgery to have a bullet removed from his chest. He lost a lot of blood and the bullet was close to his heart. Right now, there was a very real possibility that he wouldn't make it.

Dominic had asked her why she never let anyone in. Why she never bothered to get to know anyone on a personal level besides her coven. *This* was why. When you opened up to someone, gave them everything you were, you lost them. That had been her experience every single time. So, instead of feeling the agony that was gripping her heart like a vise now, she kept everyone at arm's length.

"I don't care who you think you are, if you don't get

me in to see my grandson right now, I will have you running around bleating like a goat in ten seconds. Nine. Eight."

"Shit! Grandma!" Drake jumped up from his seat and hurried across the room to where a woman stood by the front desk in the Emergency entrance where they were all gathered. Desi let go of Willow's hand and stood, taking a step as if to follow him, before stopping to glance back down at her.

"Seven. Six. Five."

The woman behind the desk was staring at her wide-eyed, backing away slowly, one hand held up in the air as if to defend herself.

"Grandma, come over here and talk to us," Drake coaxed.

"Four. Three." His grandmother didn't look like she was going to budge, and the power rolling off her in waves was impressive. There was no doubt in Willow's mind that she would follow through with her threat if the woman didn't comply. There was about to be a goat running up and down the hospital hallways.

"We need you over here, Grandma," Drake tried again.

"Mother, let's go wait with everyone else," a man who looked like Drake and Dominic said, as he walked up behind them. "I'm sure we will hear something about Dominic soon."

"Two," Victoria Hamilton snapped as she began to raise one of her hands.

"Willow needs you, Grandma. She's in pain and we don't know what to do to help her."

That got her attention when nothing else would. She glanced behind her to look over where Willow sat, Desi standing just a couple feet in front of her. Victoria's light blue eyes misted with tears, and she quickly crossed over to sit in the vacant seat by Willow. "Oh, child!"

Willow gasped when Victoria wrapped her arms around her, pulling her close, and began gently rocking her back and forth as if she really were a child. It had been so long since someone had held her this way. A sob escaped, and then another.

"It's okay, Willow. Your family is here now. We'll take care of you."

Family? She hadn't had one of those since she was eight years old. Well, except for her coven. She had gained twelve sisters when she became a part of the Sapphire Coven, but she had to admit that she was still only close to Desi, Tilly, and their cousin Arabella. It wasn't that she didn't care for the others, but she'd kept a distance between herself and them, afraid she would lose them the way she'd lost everyone else in the past.

"I can't feel him," Willow admitted, a shudder running through her body. "I can't feel him anymore."

"No!" a woman cried out. Willow raised her eyes to meet a pair of dark brown ones full of misery. She was standing next to the man who had tried to pull Victoria away from the desk just moments before. Dominic's parents, James and Eileen Hamilton. She didn't know much about them, except that they had willingly brought their only two sons to a gala not too long ago to try to get one of them to marry Desi and bind their powers with hers. That had pissed her off then, but now, looking at the very real pain in Dominic's mother's eyes, Willow was wondering if maybe she'd been wrong about her.

"I'm sorry," Willow whispered, pulling back from Victoria and bowing her head.

"You completed the bond?" Victoria asked quietly. "Bound your powers together?"

"Yes, but..." Willow hesitated, her eyes meeting Dominic's mother's again, before she looked at Victoria. "I don't know how to explain it. I still feel his magic, but I don't feel *him*."

A slow smile spread across Victoria's lips. "You need to reach deeper, Child. He's still there. I'm sure of it."

"How do you know?"

A hint of sadness crept into Victoria's eyes. "Because when my husband left to be with the Goddess, his magic left with him."

Eileen crossed the room to kneel down beside them. Reaching over, she placed her hand over the top of Willow's. "If Victoria says my son is still here, then I believe her. Let's try reaching for him together. If we join our magic with yours, it will make yours stronger and I know we will find him."

Willow had never joined her magic with anyone before, except her coven and Dominic. It wasn't done unless you fully trusted the ones involved for more than one reason. When you shared your magic with someone, it was like sharing a piece of yourself with them. They couldn't necessarily read your thoughts, but they could feel your emotions, your desires, and your fears. It was a very personal experience. Not only that, but there was always a chance that you could leave a part of your magic with them. It didn't happen often, but it could. And there was also the fear that one of the others could try to steal your magic for themselves. Willow had only heard of that happening once, but it was enough to keep her leery about who to trust that much, when trust was already an issue with her.

She didn't know Dominic's family, except for Drake. The idea of merging her magic with theirs made her nervous as hell, but she was willing to try anything if it meant being able to feel the man she loved again and know for sure that he was alive. Besides, it wasn't just *her* magic anymore. It was *theirs*. Hers and Dominic's together. He trusted his family. That was all that mattered.

The Hamiltons waited patiently for her to decide, but when Willow gave a slight nod, they wasted no time. Forming a circle, they clasped hands and Willow was happy to see Desi take a place directly across from her. She'd shared magic with her best friend numerous times over the years, and having her there went a long way towards giving her the courage to proceed.

"Once you connect with him, you need to hold on tight, Willow. You have been given a gift from the Goddess. Only you can bring him back to us."

"Wait," Willow whispered. "What do you mean bring him back? You said he was still here?"

"He is, for now." Victoria squeezed her hand gently. "Willow, you need to be strong. I believe the reason you can't feel my grandson anymore is because he is caught somewhere on a path between here and the sky above with the Goddess. If you want him back, you are going to have to fight for him. You are the only one who can. We can join our magic with yours to get you to him, but then it will be up to you."

Willow bit her lip, her gaze traveling around the room. Her coven sisters had fanned out, taking up residence around them and blocking anyone's view from what was happening. Protecting them. She met the eyes of the High Priestess, and Farrah nodded to her. "We will guard you and your family on your journey, Willow. Go now. Find the other half of your soul."

Taking a deep breath, Willow straightened her shoulders, closed her eyes, and let her magic out. She clenched her jaw hard when she felt the Hamilton's magic begin to merge with hers, and their emotions hit her. Sadness, despair, hopelessness, all coming from Dominic's mother. Worry and distress from his father. Fear and trepidation from Desi, but it was intertwined with caring and love. It was almost too much on top of what she was already feeling. Suddenly, she felt a strong burst of determination as Victoria's power collided with hers, and then Drake's hit and there was courage and confidence. It helped boost her own self-confidence and Willow found herself reaching out, searching for her lost love.

At first, there was nothing, but she refused to give up. She had finally allowed him into her life, and she wasn't letting him go. Willow pushed harder, expanding her magic, focusing on Dominic. His thick, brown hair, light blue eyes, that sexy little grin he always gave her. She searched for him, for that thread that tied them together, soul to soul, magic to magic.

"Please, Goddess, I need you," Willow whispered. "I can't lose him. Send him back to me."

There was a small tingling sensation that moved through her, and then it was gone.

Willow's heart began to race as she whispered, "You gave him to me. Our magic is bound together, along with our souls. If you take him, you better be prepared for me to follow. Wherever my love is, that is where I will be." She didn't know how Victoria had survived for so long without her husband, but somehow, she knew it wouldn't be the same for her.

"Willow, no!"

Willow ignored Desi's cry, concentrating on that tingling sensation that had returned, along with the small sliver of hope that was now coursing through her. "Send him back, Goddess. I need him. I refuse to live without him. I will fight for him to the end."

Willow felt the power within her growing and realized that it wasn't just the Hamilton's magic merging with hers. All of her coven had thrown theirs in as well. Her sisters— her family. They had thrown caution into the wind and had merged their magic with witches from another coven… for her. Willow could feel their love and devotion. They were unwilling to let Dominic go, because they refused to let her go.

"Dominic! I need you. Please, come back to me."

Willow cried out when that magical thread that she'd felt before between them was suddenly back. It tightened more and more, and then slammed back into place, strong, safe, and secure. She felt Dominic even stronger than she had before. She grasped that thread tightly, holding it to her, refusing to ever let it slip away again.

He fought to stay with you. Even though I welcomed him here with me, he wouldn't leave you. You have had so much taken from you, My Child. You deserve happiness. You deserve to love and be loved. Stop holding back from those who care for you. Let them in. Care for them. Love them.

Willow felt a tear slip down her cheek, followed by

another. She knew that voice. She wasn't sure how she'd never heard it before, but she knew who it belonged to.

"Thank you for your gift, Goddess," she whispered. "I will do as you say. I promise."

Your parents and brother are safe with me, Willow. You will see them again someday, but for now, your place is beside Dominic, and with your family and friends.

A sob caught in her throat, and Willow rasped, "I miss them so much."

They are always with you, My Child, as am I. You must go now. But, Willow, take care. The man with the gun is nearby. Watching her. He is always watching her.

Willow frowned in confusion, then swallowed hard. "Watching who? Is it Derek, Goddess? Was he the one who shot Dominic?"

That man is always watching you, but he didn't pull the trigger. It was the other one. The one after your sister.

Willow's eyes sprang open when she felt her connection to the Goddess disappear. Her gaze went quickly around the room, aware of the faces surrounding her. Their magic had also dissipated, returning to them and leaving her alone with just hers and Dominic's swirling around inside her. Her Dominic. He was alive, she could feel him. The Goddess had given him back to her, and she was never letting him go.

"Did you really just have a conversation with the freaking Goddess?" Tilly whispered in awe.

"Either that, or she was talking to herself," Raelyn said dryly.

"She does talk in her sleep sometimes," Desi told them.

"She told me whoever hurt Dominic is close," Willow

interrupted, looking out the window next to Brinley. "And it wasn't Derek. There's someone else who is out there and always watching *her*."

"Always watching who?"

"I'm not sure. One of my sisters, was all she would say." Someone in my coven was in trouble, but I had no idea who.

"What about my son?" Dominic's mother cut in. "Is he okay?"

Willow's eyes widened as she realized she had been so focused on the threat to one of her sisters, that she'd failed to share the best news yet. A wide grin crossed her face as she brought her hand up to rest on her chest. "Yes! I feel him again! Even more than I did before."

"Thank the Goddess," his mother whispered, swiping at the tears that were forming in her eyes. "Thank you, Willow. We owe you more than we can ever repay you."

Willow shook her head, intertwining her fingers with the woman. "No, you don't owe me anything. We're family now. That's what family does."

It was her first step to accepting others into her heart. She'd made a promise to the Goddess, and she never broke a promise.

CHAPTER TEN

Dominic sat in front of the fireplace holding Willow close. He'd been out of the hospital for over two weeks now, and she hadn't left his side. They started out at his house, but there was no privacy with his parents and grandmother walking in and out of his room constantly to check on him. Finally, when he couldn't stand it anymore, he'd packed a bag, and they went to Willow's so they could finally have some privacy. The place where he was hoping to call home soon, if she would have him.

It was Christmas Eve, a night he normally spent with family, but not this year. Tonight was special, and just for the two of them.

"You asked me one time why I never let anyone close." Willow's voice was so low, he had to lower his head closer to hers to hear it. "You were right, I don't."

Dominic could tell whatever she was about to say was painful for her, and he cupped her chin, tilting her head up until she met his gaze. "You don't have to tell me anything you don't want to, baby."

Her eyelids lowered, her long lashes fluttering before she opened her eyes to look at him again. "I had a brother. His name was William." She hesitated, then whispered, "He was my twin. My best friend. We did everything together. I lost him to cancer when we were seven. By the time the doctors found out about it, it was too late."

"Shit, Willow. I'm so sorry."

Willow laid her head on his shoulder, her forehead resting against his neck. "A year later, my parents died in a car accident. They were the only family I had, so I was sent to live in foster care. No one wanted a messed up eight-year-old child, so there was no chance at adoption. I was quiet, sullen, angry."

"Of course, you were. You just lost everyone you loved."

"Potential parents don't care why you act the way you do, Dominic. They just want a perfect, ready-made family, and I didn't fit in the picture of those families."

Dominic stayed quiet, even though he wanted nothing more than to argue and tell her how wonderful she was, and how any family would have been lucky to have her. He knew she needed to talk through the pain he could feel radiating from her.

"When I was in seventh grade, I turned my life around. I began to get straight A's instead of C's and D's. I was determined to make something of myself, because everyone I knew didn't think I could. I ended up with a full ride scholarship to college, where I met Jenny. She was older than me by a couple of years, but when we met, we just clicked—besties from the start."

The flames in the fireplace crackled loudly, and a piece of wood fell off another, causing it to roll close to the edge of the grate. Dominic casually waved his hand, moving it back to decrease the danger of a fire in the living room.

"She was assaulted one night on the way home from studying at the library. I was supposed to be with her but stayed in my dorm room because I wasn't feeling well." Willow's hand clenched the front of his shirt tightly as she whispered, "They beat her pretty badly and left her in an alley. She didn't make it."

Dominic placed a gentle kiss on the top of her head, then rubbed his chin against it. Hell, no wonder she was so wary about getting close to anyone.

"After that, I shut down. I refused to make friends. I kept to myself. I went to school and work, that was it."

"Until you met Desi?" he guessed.

Willow nodded, her grip on his shirt loosening. "Yes. That woman is so damn stubborn, she wouldn't let me block her out."

Dominic grinned, thankful to his sister-in-law for her tenacity. "I'm glad."

"She felt my magic. She said it called to her, and she knew we were destined to be best friends and for me to be a part of her coven."

"I've heard of that happening before," Dominic admitted.

"Well, after six months of her constantly badgering me, I finally caved," Willow said, looking up at him and grinning. "Best decision I ever made!"

"Oh yeah?" he teased, placing a soft kiss on her lips. "That's the best one?"

Willow's cheeks flushed a deep pink, and she ducked her head. "One of the best ones."

"So, that's what you meant about me not leaving you like everyone else?"

"You heard that, did you?" Willow murmured, sliding a hand up under his sweater to rest it over his heart as she leaned her head back down on his shoulder.

"I did."

Willow was quiet for a moment, and then she nodded. "Yes, it is. Everyone I've ever loved has died."

"Except for Desi," Dominic muttered, moving his hand down to slip it under her shirt, so that he could touch her soft skin.

"And you."

Dominic froze, sure he'd heard wrong. Willow had never hinted at loving him, even after he was shot, so he'd kept his feelings to himself, afraid to ruin the closeness they now had.

"It nearly killed me when you were hurt, Dominic," she whispered, her fingers sliding through the hair on his chest. "I thought I lost you. Even merged with your family, I couldn't find you at first."

"Wait, what are you talking about?" Dominic asked in confusion, pulling back from her, so he could look in her eyes. "You merged your magic with my family's? Why would you do that?" He couldn't imagine his Willow merging her magic with anyone, and giving them any kind of power over her, except him. And, if he was honest, he still couldn't believe she chose to bind their powers together the way they had.

"Your family never told you?"

Dominic slowly shook his head, his brow furrowing as he thought back. "No. No one mentioned anything."

Willow's hand went to his chest again, right over his

heart. She touched him there a lot now, as if it made her feel more connected to him. "I couldn't feel you, Dominic. When you were in the hospital, I sat in that waiting room and tried so damn hard, but no matter what I did, I couldn't *feel* you."

"Oh, baby." He couldn't imagine what that would be like. Ever since their bond had snapped into place, he'd felt her. If she was happy, sad, or pissed off, he knew.

Willow's breath caught as she rasped, "Your grandmother said it was because you were on a path between our world and the Goddess."

"I was dying."

"Yes." Willow's big, green eyes filled with tears. "I couldn't let you go, Dominic. If you did, I would have followed."

"Willow, no."

"We are tied together by the Goddess for eternity. I couldn't have stayed here without you." Before he could reply, she went on, "Your mother had the idea of merging our magic together so I would have more power to try to connect with you."

"You did that willingly?"

"I would do anything for you," Willow said softly. "But it didn't work, not until my sisters joined their magic with ours."

"Holy shit." He couldn't imagine the amount of power that had to have been running through the hospital that night.

"It worked." Willow's chin quivered, a slow smile tilting up the corners of her mouth. "I found you, and the Goddess gave you back to me."

"Remind me to thank her," Dominic muttered, his hand going to caress the curve of her cheek.

"She told me that I deserve to love and be loved."

"She's right," Dominic whispered, lowering his lips to hers. "I love you, Willow Ryder. So damn much."

"I love you, too, Dom. Enough to follow you into death."

"Fuck, baby, you say the sweetest things."

Dominic claimed her mouth with his, slipping his tongue past her lips to find hers. He groaned, sliding his hands up under her shirt and over her back until he came to the clasp of her bra. He made short work of undoing it, then broke the kiss and leaned back to remove both her shirt and bra.

It was the first time since he'd come home that they'd shared more than a few kisses, and he wasn't holding back. He needed her. He was done waiting.

Dominic felt Willow's hands sliding his T-shirt up, and he moved quickly to help her slip it off. He wanted to feel those hands gliding all over his body, her skin flush against his. It had been too long since he was inside her —loving her.

"Dominic," she breathed, her hands going to cup her breasts, flicking her own nipples. It was so fucking hot; he almost came in his pants like a teenager.

Dominic pushed the yoga pants she was wearing down and off, along with her panties, his jeans quickly following. As soon as he had them off, Willow threw her leg over his hips, straddling him. Her mouth found his, her hand going to his thick erection. He groaned when she positioned his cock at her wet entrance and began to lower herself down onto him.

"Fuck, this isn't going to last long," he warned, unable to stop himself from arching up into her, burying himself in her wet heat. "I wanted to go slow with you, Willow. Show you how much you mean to me. How much I love you—need you."

"I already know all of that," Willow growled, grasping the back of the couch as she began to ride him. "Right now, I just need you to move!"

That he could do. Dominic wrapped his hands around her hips and pushed up into her, matching the rhythm she set. Her breasts were bouncing in front of him, and he couldn't stop himself from tasting her. Sucking her nipple inside his mouth, he played with it with his tongue, loving the way it felt.

"Dominic!" Willow cried, her breath coming out raggedly as she moved up and down on his dick. "I'm so close!"

Dominic let go of her nipple and thrust deeper—harder into her. "Come for me, baby," he demanded. "You feel so fucking good."

Willow screamed Dominic's name as her pussy convulsed around him, pulling his own orgasm from him. It started with a tingling at the base of his spine, then his balls drew up and he unloaded inside of her. His Willow. His life.

They sat like that in front of the fire for several minutes, Dominic still buried deep inside her, before he kissed her gently and pulled back to look at her. "I know this probably isn't the best time, but I can't wait any longer, Willow."

"The best time for what?" Willow asked in confusion

as she ran her hands over his shoulders and down to rest on his upper arms.

Dominic opened his hand, palm up in front of her, and a small, dark blue velvet box appeared. "It's unconventional, but so are we."

"What?"

Willow slowly took the box from him and opened it, gasping at the large sapphire surrounded by several small diamonds.

"It was my great grandmother's," Dominic said, removing it from the box. "It was given to me when she passed away to give to the woman I chose to spend the rest of my life with." Taking her hand in his, he slowly slid it on her ring finger. "I choose you."

A tremulous smile crossed Willow's lips as she whispered, "I choose you too, Dominic."

CHAPTER ELEVEN

Willow took one last look at where Dominic stood by his car waiting for her. He leaned back against it, arms crossed over his thick chest, a small grin on his face. He'd wanted to come inside with her, but this was something she needed to do herself. She had to show the other attorneys in the law firm that she was strong and capable, in case things went the way she was pretty positive they were going to, and she ended up being pitted against any of them in court in the future.

Inhaling deeply, Willow turned and climbed the stairs of the old building where Johnson and Johnson Law Firm had their offices on the fourth floor. They'd been there since before Willow came to work for them and would probably still be there ten years down the road. The outside was older, but the inside was all remodeled and immaculate.

Willow nodded to the security guard who sat at the front desk before making her way over to the elevators.

Stepping inside, she punched the button to the fourth floor and waited impatiently for the doors to shut. She was praying Derek was on vacation still. It was New Year's Eve, so he shouldn't be back in town yet, but he'd been so unpredictable lately, she wasn't sure he even left town. She just wanted to go in, talk to Mr. Johnson, and grab whatever she needed to from her office, and then leave again.

The doors were just about closed when a hand appeared, prying them open. Willow cringed inwardly when the man himself stepped in, caging her up against the back of the elevator as the door closed behind him. When it started to rise, he reached back and punched the button that made it stop, suspended between floors.

"Willow, it's nice to see you."

Willow's nose scrunched up when the smell of whiskey filled the air. "Derek, are you drunk?"

He leaned in closer, and Willow let out a small squeak of surprise when he wrapped one of his hands around her neck as if to hold her in place. "You've been ignoring my phone calls, Willow."

It was true. She'd received several calls over the last couple of weeks from both Derek's cell phone and the work number and had ignored every single one of them. She'd been focusing on Dominic and didn't have time for Derek's games.

"I suggest you get your hands off me, Derek."

He wasn't hurting her, just trying to intimidate her. Unfortunately for him, she wasn't afraid of him anymore. She had Dominic on her side, along with her magic. Derek Johnson couldn't hurt her. She doubted he even had the balls to try. He was just a dirty old man who had fixated on her for some reason. Well, that was going to change after today or she would slap a restraining order on him so fast it would make his head spin.

"What are you going to do if I don't?"

A slow smile spread over Willow's face as she cocked her head to the side and lifted an eyebrow. Her gaze going to the buttons behind him, she narrowed her eyes on the number four. Pushing her power lightly toward it, satisfaction filled her when the light behind it lit up and the elevator started to move again.

"This is your last chance, Derek," she warned, her gaze meeting his.

"How the fuck did you do that?" Derek demanded, his eyes darkening in anger.

"Magic," Willow whispered, as the doors opened behind him, showing his grandfather waiting in front of them, probably to take the elevator down to go to lunch.

"You fucking witch," Derek snarled, so pissed with her that he was unaware that they were drawing a crowd. "You can't ignore me. I will do whatever I want to you whenever I want."

"And if I say no?"

"You won't."

Willow wanted to laugh at the spectacle the jackass was making of himself, but she couldn't. Not yet. "And why is that?"

"Because, I will make sure you never make partner if you do."

"You see, that's where your problem lies," Willow said, meeting his grandfather's gaze over his shoulder. "I have no desire to be a part of this law firm anymore, partner or not. My resignation is in your email, Mr. Johnson. I believe Derek just made it perfectly clear as to why."

Derek froze, before slowly lowering his hand from her neck and turning to look at his grandfather. Willow didn't wait for either of them to say anything. She slid past him and left the elevator, stalking down the hall to her office. This might be the last time she was ever in this building, but it wouldn't be the last time she practiced law. She already had three interviews scheduled with various law firms in the city, and she refused to settle for anything less than what she wanted. She had a lot of money saved up and didn't need to work if she didn't want to. She worked because she enjoyed what she did, and she loved helping others.

Willow stood in the doorway of her office, her gaze skimming around the room, before she realized there was nothing of importance that she wanted to take with her. Her briefcase was already at home, and she had no personal items. No pictures, or plants, or special notebooks and pens. Nothing. The office was as stale as her life used to be before Dominic walked into it.

After one last look, she turned around and left. Derek and his grandfather were still standing in front of the elevators, and it looked like they'd been arguing. Derek's face was dark red, and Mr. Johnson's held a thunderous expression.

"Willow, I don't know what my nincompoop of a grandson did this time, but we do not want you to leave. We were actually just getting ready to offer you a partner position in the company."

He didn't know what his grandson did? Wasn't he just standing in front of the elevator when Derek showed his douchebag side with his threats and his hand around her throat?

"Thank you, Sir, but it's a little late for that."

When he frowned, Willow stepped into the elevator and pushed the button for the main floor. "Thank you for the opportunity you gave me with Johnson and Johnson, Sir. I will always appreciate it."

"Dammit, Willow! You can't just leave like this! I had plans for us."

"Those were your plans, Derek, not mine."

"Willow!"

When he started to come toward her, Willow couldn't help herself. The doors were almost shut when she waved her hand toward him. His belt buckle came undone, along with his pants, and they fell to his ankles, showing the black velvet thong he wore beneath them. There was muffled laughter as he struggled to pull his pants back up, and Willow waved as the doors closed on his shocked gaze. She was sure he wouldn't follow, not after she gave him a little hint of her power.

A peacefulness filled Willow when she walked out of the front doors of the building, and she saw Dominic there waiting for her. She walked over to him and right into his awaiting arms. This was what it felt like to love and be loved. If it wasn't for the Goddess above, she never would have given herself the chance to find out. Raising her head, she sent a silent thank you above.

"You okay?" Dominic asked, as he lowered his head to kiss her gently on the lips.

Willow smiled. "More than okay."

"Let's go home, love."

Willow wrapped her arms around his neck and kissed him again. "I love you, Dom."

"Love you too, baby."

OTHER BOOKS BY DAWN SULLIVAN

RARE Series

Book 1 Nico's Heart

Book 2 Phoenix's Fate

Book 3 Trace's Temptation

Book 4 Saving Storm

Book 5 Angel's Destiny

Book 6 Jaxson's Justice

Book 7 Rikki's Awakening

White River Wolves Series

Book 1 Josie's Miracle

Book 2 Slade's Desire

Book 3 Janie's Salvation

Book 4 Sable's Fire

Serenity Springs Series

Book 1 Tempting His Heart

Book 2 Healing Her Spirit

Book 3 Saving His Soul

Book 4 A Caldwell Wedding

Book 5 Keeping Her Trust

Alluring Assassins

Book 1 Cassia

Sass and Growl

Book 1 His Bunny Kicks Sass

Book 2 Protecting His Fox's Sass

Book 3 Accepting His Witch's Sass

Book 4 Chasing His Lynx's Sass

Chosen By Destiny

Book 1 Blayke

Book 2 Bellame

Magical Mojo

Book 1 Witch Way To Love

Rogue Enforcers

Karma

Dark Leopards West Texas Chapter

Book 1 Shadow's Revenge

Book 7 Demon's Hellfire

Standalone

Wedding Bell Rock

The De La Vega Familia Trilogy (Social Rejects Syndicate)

Book 1 Tomas

Make sure and visit my website for information on all of my books, and to sign up for my Newsletter where you will receive all of the latest information on new releases, sales, and more!

Website: **http://www.dawnsullivanauthor.com/**

I would love to have you join my reader's group, Author Dawn Sullivan's Rebel Readers, so that we can hang out and chat, and where you will also get sneak peeks of cover reveals, read excerpts before anyone else, and more!

https://www.facebook.com/groups/AuthorDawnSullivansRebelReaders/

ABOUT THE AUTHOR

Dawn Sullivan has a wonderful, supportive husband, and three beautiful children. She enjoys spending time with them, which normally involves some baseball, shooting hoops, taking walks, watching movies, and reading.

Her passion for reading began at a very young age and only grew over time. Whether she was bringing home a book from the library or sneaking one of her mother's romance novels to read by the light in the hallway when she was supposed to be sleeping, Dawn always had a book. She reads several different genres and subgenres, but Paranormal Romance and Romantic Suspense are her favorites.

Dawn has always made up stories of her own, and finally decided to start sharing them with others. She hopes everyone enjoys reading them as much as she enjoys writing them.